MR. MEN
Rainy Day
Roger Hargreaves

Hello, my name is Walter. Can you spot me in this book?

Original concept by
Roger Hargreaves

Written and illustrated by
Adam Hargreaves

EGMONT

"It's a disaster!" cried Little Miss Splendid, when she opened her curtains to see that it was pouring with rain.

The rain was going to spoil her special day out.

How was anyone going to have any fun if they were stuck inside all day?

It was not going to be the splendid day out that she had hoped for.

It was going to be a boring day in!

Where was the fun in that?

And then Little Miss Fun arrived.

"It's a disaster!" cried Little Miss Splendid.

"Nonsense!" said Little Miss Fun. "There are plenty of fun things to do inside on a rainy day."

"Do you really think so?" asked Little Miss Splendid, hopefully.

"Better than that, I know so!" cried Little Miss Fun. "Now, leave it all to me."

Soon all Little Miss Splendid's friends started to arrive.
Mr Forgetful had forgotten his umbrella and his
wellingtons had filled with water.

What a soggy mess!

Little Miss Fun ran round the house in a whirl of organisation, finding things for everyone to do.

Mr Nonsense and Little Miss Scatterbrain were left to bake a cake in the kitchen.

Little Miss Fun took Little Miss Star and Little Miss Giggles up to Little Miss Splendid's bedroom to play dressing up.

Mr Mischief and Little Miss Naughty were given board games to play in the hallway.

Mr Forgetful and Little Miss Somersault found themselves in the living room with cardboard and string and glue to make things.

And Little Miss Fun led Little Miss Dotty and Mr Dizzy to the dining room where she had provided paper and paints for them.

"There you go," she said to Little Miss Splendid. "Everyone has something fun to do!"

And as the rain continued to fall, everyone did have fun. Although not quite in the way that Little Miss Splendid and Little Miss Fun had imagined it ...

Mr Nonsense and Little Miss Scatterbrain didn't make one cake, they made lots and lots of cakes. Lots and lots of crazy, daft cakes.

They made a banana and pea cake.

They made a lemon and sausage cake.

They made a strawberry and toothpaste cake.

And they even made a blueberry, chocolate, pickle and onion cake!

None of which were at all nice to eat, but fantastic to look at.

Which is more than could be said for Little Miss Splendid's kitchen.

Making all those crazy, daft cakes involved a crazy, daft mess!

"My beautiful kitchen!" spluttered Little Miss Splendid.

And then she heard cries of delight coming from the living room.

She ran to see what was going on, but soon wished she hadn't.

Mr Forgetful and Little Miss Somersault had suspended her very expensive rug from her very valuable chandelier with string and were playing magic carpet rides.

And they had glued her antique chairs together to make a ladder to reach their magic carpet.

"My glorious rug!" screeched Little Miss Splendid.

And then she heard screams of excitement coming from the hallway.

Mr Mischief and Little Miss Naughty had got bored of the board games and were now using the boards like sledges to slide down the stairs and across the hallway, crashing into all her precious vases as they went.

CRASH!

CRASH!

CRASH!

"My precious vases!" gasped Little Miss Splendid.

And then two fantastically dressed figures appeared at the top of the stairs wearing Little Miss Splendid's smartest hats all covered in feathers.

Little Miss Giggles and Little Miss Star had been pillow fighting!

And then the dining room door swung open to reveal Mr Dizzy and Little Miss Dotty who had decided to redecorate the walls.

Little Miss Splendid's very splendid dining room looked like the inside of a circus tent!

Poor Little Miss Splendid. But at least all her friends had a good time which goes to show that there are lots of things that you can do to have fun on a rainy day.

But there are, of course, some things that you can't do on a rainy day...

Out in the garden, sat in the rain was Mr Muddle...

... sunbathing!